Copyright © 2002 by Nord-Süd Verlag AG, Gossau Zürich, Switzerland
First published in Switzerland under the title *Alex war's!*
English translation © 2002 by North-South Books Inc., New York

First published in the United States, Great Britain, Canada,
Australia, and New Zealand in 2002 by North-South Books,
an imprint of Nord-Süd Verlag AG, Gossau Zürich, Switzerland.

Distributed in the United States by North-South Books Inc., New York.

Library of Congress Cataloging-in-Publication Data is available.
A CIP catalogue record for this book is available from The British Library.
ISBN 0-7358-1578-X (trade edition) 10 9 8 7 6 HC 5 4 3 2 1
ISBN 0-7358-1579-8 (library edition) 10 9 8 7 6 LE 5 4 3 2 1

For more information about our books, and the authors and artists
who create them, visit our web site: www.northsouth.com

Printed in Germany

Alex Did It!

BY UDO WEIGELT

ILLUSTRATED BY
CRISTINA KADMON

TRANSLATED BY J. ALISON JAMES

North-South Books
NEW YORK • LONDON

Bouncer, Buster, and Baby were three little
hares who loved to romp wildly through the
woods. One day they made so much noise that
they woke up Bear, who was napping in his tree.

Bear stormed out angrily. "Who was that? Who
woke me up? Who was making all that noise?"
he growled.

The three little hares shrank back in fear.

Then, suddenly, Bouncer piped up, "Alex did it! It wasn't us! We just happened to be passing by at the same time. Believe me!"

"Alex? Who on earth is Alex?" asked Bear.

"Alex is a hare, and he is new in the forest. I'm sure he didn't mean to wake you," said Bouncer. "As soon as he heard you, he ran away fast!"

"I see," said Bear, and grumbling, he turned back to his hole.

Relieved, the three hopped on.

"Wow, Bouncer! That was a great idea!" cried Buster.

"What idea?" asked Baby. "And who is Alex anyway? Did he wake up the bear or did we? I don't know any Alex."

"Of course you don't," Bouncer said. "I just made him up! Now anytime we get into trouble, we can just say that Alex did it!"

This meant they could do anything they wanted to do. They spied on Squirrel to find where she buried her nuts for the winter. Then as soon as her back was turned, they dug up her nuts and had a little snack.

When Squirrel came back and saw that all her nuts were gone, Bouncer quickly said, "Alex did it! He's a new hare around here. He ran off when he saw you coming."

Next they played a trick on Badger. They stuffed the entrance to his hole with leaves.

When Badger woke up from his nap, he was astonished. It was dark already! Had he slept all day, he wondered? Then, when he tried to get out of his hole, he had to dig and dig through a huge mountain of leaves. "What a rude trick!" he said angrily when he finally emerged.

"Alex did it!" said Buster. "He's a new hare in the forest. And he just ran off."

The hares ran away giggling and started a game of tag. In their leaping and diving they tore apart Rabbit's whole vegetable garden.

When Rabbit saw the damage, she glared at the three little hares. "Alex did it!" Baby said sweetly. "Alex is a new hare in the forest. He just ran off."

Whatever trouble the three little hares got into, Alex was to blame. Even when they got home late and their mother scolded them, they told her it was Alex's fault. Alex was becoming famous in the forest. All the animals were mad at him, but nobody was mad at the three mischievous hares—Bouncer, Buster, and Baby.

The next morning, as Bouncer, Buster, and Baby were hopping along, they met a strange new hare.

"Hello," he called out cheerfully. "I'm new here in the forest. My name is Alex. What are your names?"

"Wha . . . what? Your name is ALEX?" Bouncer asked, astonished. "That's terrible!"

"Why? What's wrong with my name?" asked the new hare.

Bouncer, Buster, and Baby were very embarrassed when they told Alex what they'd been doing.

"But that's awful!" Alex cried. "My name really *is* Alex. I can't just turn into someone different."

Bouncer, Buster, and Baby looked at each other.

"There's nothing else to do," sighed Buster.

The three little hares hung their ears and slowly hopped off. Alex followed along behind them, wondering what they were up to.

They found Bear and told him the truth.

"I see," said Bear. "Well, Alex, to welcome you to the forest, I'll give you a big pawful of berries. But those three get nothing!"

Bouncer, Buster, and Baby made their way through the whole forest.

All the animals were mad at the three little hares. But Alex got welcoming presents from everyone—carrots from Rabbit, nuts from Squirrel, mushrooms from Badger, and much, much more. Alex got enough treats to fill up two big leaves.

Finally the three little hares finished telling everyone about their lies.

"I don't ever want to have another day like this," moaned Bouncer.

"I'd rather tie my ears in a knot," agreed Buster.

"Not me!" Alex laughed. "I got so many presents. And now, thanks to you, all the animals know me. I'm grateful. So let's have a picnic and share all these treats."

The four little hares had a wonderful afternoon eating and playing and eating some more. The only problem was that Bouncer, Buster, and Baby got home late again. But they didn't blame it on Alex, even though this time it really was true!